Achintya Gupta

The Tomitaro

A Devil's Labyrinth

The Tomitaro - A Devil's Labyrinth

BY
Achintya Gupta

Price : Rs. 99/-

ISBN : 978-81-949078-3-1

Printed & Published by   :   **Foil Printers**, Ludhiana
0161-2404979, 2404093
www.foilprintersludhiana.com

About the Author

Achintya Gupta, just turned 9, living in Ludhiana, Punjab, is currently studying in Grade 4 in Sat Paul Mittal School, Ludhiana.

He has a fetish for reading. Also fond of playing guitar, he is into his guitar practice. He is into computer coding and has an instinct for Badminton as well.

Achintya loves to spend time with his grandparents, parents, and his elder brother. He is emotionally linked to his family. He says: "I am thankful, first to Almighty Lord, and then to my grandparents, Mr. Ashok Kumar Gupta, Advocate and Mrs. Rachna Gupta. I have immense gratitude for my parents, CA Arun Gupta and Mrs. Mansi Gupta, who have been with me through everything. My elder brother, Akshat Gupta, is my back support who pushes me to pursue my dreams."

Achintya can be reached at
achintya.gupta2011@gmail.com

LET US BEGIN....

CHAPTER-1

Shifting of House

6th October 2020, Fedrick Vought, a sincere boy, woke up at 7:30 AM. He was shifting to a new house along with his parents. His parents, Joe and Mary, were busy packing the stuff . Fedrick jumped at a snap from his bed, hurtling. He started packing his bags too. Mary called Fedrick to eat his breakfast. He rapidly ate his breakfast and went off to his room. As all the packing was done, they kept the bags in the van and started their Journey. When they reached the destination, they were all excited to see their new house. Near the house was a meadow. At the bottom of the meadow was a running brook and at the top of the meadow grew a grove of fir trees. There was a pond and at the side grew rushes and water lilies.

CHAPTER-2

A Mysterious Letter

After dinner, the family went to sleep.Fedrick's bedroom was upstairs. While he slept, the door cracked open and a man entered the house. With a letter in his hand, he went upstairs towards Fedrick's bedroom. When he reached the bedroom, he threw the letter in the room and quickly made off. Frederick's mother heard a noise and ran to check. But the man was gone. Fedrick also woke suddenly and saw the letter. He was surprised to see the letter lying on the floor. He wore his specs and started reading the crumbly letter.

MR.FEDRICK VOUGHT,

I AM PLEASED TO INFORM YOU THAT YOU ARE SELECTED TO TAKE THE TREASURE! YOU ARE REQUESTED TO JUST WEAR THE RING KEPT IN THE LETTER. WHEN YOU WEAR THE RING, FIRST YOU WOULD FIND THAT YOU ARE IN A STRANGE WORLD BUT VERY NEAR, YOU WOULD FIND TREASURE.

WHEN YOU GET THE TREASURE, TAKE THE RING OUT OF YOUR FINGER. THEN YOU WOULD SEE THAT YOU ARE BACK AT YOUR HOME. AFTER THAT, DESTROY THE RING WITHOUT WEARING IT.

The man who had written the letter hadn't written his name on the letter. Fedrick was very excited. He wore the ring. First, the letter was said correctly and he entered a cave. He saw a sword and shield. He was wondering whether these two things only were the treasure. He grabbed both the things and some writing came in the air.

"WELCOME TO THE GAME 'TOMITARO'. WHEN YOU FINISH THIS GAME , JUST SAY 'TOMITARO'

CHAPTER-3

The Journey Starts

Fedrick was surprised to see the words written and had never seen anything like that before. He grabbed the sword and the shield. But he couldn't understand the second line. It said *"Finish the Game"*. He then, after wandering for quite a significant period of time, realized that the letter was playing pranks on him! Huge undeniably scary Pranks! He checked his arms; he saw that he had strong muscles now. He also saw some tattoos drawn on his arms. First was a Serpent, second was a Lion and third was a Wand drawn. The rest of the body was same, but on the arms he was bit modified. He instinctively wanted to go back home. So he took off the ring from his finger but nothing happened, he was still entrapped in the cave. He shouted, cried and tried to run out from the cave. He tried his best to make back home, but couldn't. While he was running here and there to get out of the cave , suddenly an ugly looking man popped up in front of him. Fedrick was scared to death. After a moment of experiencing adrenaline in his veins, he came to senses and interrogated , 'Who are you ?'.

The other person replied,'I am your way to death!' I am a reflection of what you do not want. I am scary, I am horror, I am death. I am your pathway to the ultimate rest of your life- the death.

Fedrick stared at him and said, 'Oh! Is that so?' He raised his sword and shield.

The other person also had a sword and shield. Now Fedrick was scared again. He felt like something was trapping him in the unwanted circle of fear.The ugly man hit him by the sword. Fedrick's head was now separated from his body. But to his emotional surprise, he found his head back in its place.

'I am alive !' exclaimed Fedrick. Fedrick's fear started to calm down and his senses were coming back to him. Now Fedrick was not scared at all. He started fighting. But the shabby person knew his sword skills and was ready to encounter Fedrick.Fedrick was also defending maturely with his shield. Fedrick boxed him hard on his face and kicked him on his stomach. The man started bleeding. The man felt very weak and at last Fedrick hit him with his sword and the man was not alive anymore. Fredrick felt a sense of victory.

CHAPTER-4

The Powers of Federick

Fedrick was confused about how his head was back to normal while fighting. He looked at tattoos made on his arm, he realized that each tattoo had different powers. He thought about the game intelligently to figure out exactly what was going on. He began to make sense of the game, of what it was all about.He dozed off and woke up after 45 minutes only to see two men taking something with them. He decided to follow them one meter far away. He was trying to conceal himself from the men when to his surprise, he suddenly transformed into a serpent. His two weapons were gone .He followed the two men who were taking something. The men were going towards a hall with enormous walls. Fedrick (Serpent) entered the hall. He saw there were people performing strange scientific things. He went forward and saw the chemical in the test tubes. There were discussions going on, about testing the chemical on animals. They saw Fedrick, disguised as Serpent and caught it. They figured out a plan to test the chemical on the victim that had himself arrived at their place and finally tested the chemical on the serpent.The serpent died and it meant that Fedrick died. However Fedrick came back again. He now understood one thing about the tattoo,it was his life count. It meant that now he had the powers of the Lion. He planned to kill those people and then spill out the whole illegal scientific performance. He transformed into a lion and entered the hall and successfully executed his plan . He came to an understanding that in this game, *Tomitaro*, there are levels. He transformed into a normal human being again.

CHAPTER-5

The Intelligent Hag

Fedrick was feeling a little monotonous of walking around. Nothing adventurous was happening with him. He started evaluating his powers. He could transform into a Lion, could take out claws,had the ability to jump, could run fast and could growl. He was practicing to use his powers, when suddenly incessant wind started blowing. Fedrick knew that something dangerous was coming. Suddenly a lady with a wand was standing in front of him. Fedrick transformed himself into a lion and growled. The Hag's wand fell from her hand. She picked her wand and casted a spell. But Fedrick jumped high and got ready to eschew her by his claws. When he was coming to hit her, the Hag spelled, *"Imblebelio!"*.

Fedrick was in her control now and she picked him up and threw him away.Fedrick was hurt.He tried to encounter her and win but he couldn't.

CHAPTER-6

Spells

Fedrick was very tired and he fell unconscious. The hag thought that he was dead, so she moved away. But Fedrick, awoke, he jumped abruptly. He looked for the hag here and there but she was gone. Fedrick decided to formulate a plan to defeat her. Just then a man, riding a horse, came towards him. His name was Salazar. Fedrick growled and got ready to defend himself but Salazar was there to help.

Salazar said, 'Hey!dont hurt me, I'm here to help you!'

Fedrick was puzzled and transformed back to normal.

'Prove it.' Said Fedrick.

Salazar then gave him a book to defeat the hag.

'Thank You very much', said Fedrick happily. 'Now we'll together defeat the hag.'said Fedrick.

Salazar smiled and nodded. Fedrick turned the page and saw how the hag was born and how to defeat her. There were some spells written too and the powers that spells had:-

1. 'Bombshot' – Bombs would be coming out from the wand.

1. 'Ickle Tickle' – Enemy will automatically start to laugh.

1. 'Freezium' – The enemy will be freezed (Freezy Jinx)

1. 'Lampon' – Light will come out from the wand in your hand.

1. 'Tremendous' – Used for an eclipse, snakes

1. 'Firelight' – A beam of light would come out of your wand and hit the enemy.

1. 'Farnum' – Same thing would happen as in Firelight Spell.

1. 'Vanishium' – The enemy or thing would vanish.

1. 'Mike Locke' – The sound of the man would become loud.

1. 'Pushback' – Knocks down the enemy. (Knock back jinx)

Salazar told Fedrick how to cast and move a wand in each spell. Frederick practiced as hard as he could. Then he read the book further. There were spells for flying also:-

1. *'Boogie-Woogie'* – Point the wand towards yourself and say the spell loudly.

1. *'Broomstick'* – A Broomstick is also used for flying.

Then Fedrick suddenly found a wand in the book.

CHAPTER-7

The Fight Continues

Fedrick and Salazar looked for the Hag everywhere but weren't able to find her. Fedrick looked up in the air. He saw something flying, an object coming nearer and nearer. He realized that it was the Hag flying on a Dragon.

'Ha Ha',laughed the witch. 'I would defeat you kids', she growled.

Fedrick casted the Freezy Jinx- *'Frisium !'*

Then the Hag freezed and fell off from the dragon. She wasn't dead yet.

'I am gonna kill you little ones, ' said the hag.

'You wish, replied Fedrick.

The witch turned angrily and made an eclipse.

'An Eclipse !, Help me !' exclaimed Salazar

Fedrick thought and reminded himself of the time when he was learning spells.

'Yes! I know the spell' – *'Tremendous'*, shouted Fedrick.

The eclipse suddenly vanished.

'You two fools!' growled the witch. *'Firelight'* casted the Hag.

Fedrick was hurt. But he stood up and casted the spell *'Farnum'*.

The witch casted *'Ickle-Tickle'*.

Fedrick's grip was losing. He grasped the wand with both the hands. The Hag's wand was out of her hand and the two spells mixed and hit her. Suddenly her hat fell from her head and then something happened to the hag.

Fedrick realized that in reality, the hag was just a normal woman. He was surprised. It was the time to finish her.

'Avra ka Davra' muttered Fedrick and the hag was finished.

CHAPTER-8

Serpent

Fedrick was glad to see hag dead. After that Fedrick went with Salazar riding on a horse. While going they saw a trunk, an enormous trunk. Fedrick and Salazar exclaimed 'Treasure!'.

Fedrick ran in a hurry.

'Wait', said Salazar. 'First do the knockback jinx on it' he said.

'Okay! *Pushback*' exclaimed Fedrick.

The trunk opened. A snake was in there. Fedrick was scared.

'Run!' said Fedrick. They jumped on the horse and rode away fast.

Fedrick casted the spells but the snake was very fast. He couldn't do anything but had to run. The snake suddenly leapt on Fedrick.

'Fedrick! Cast a spell' shouted Salazar.

'I want to go to the washroom' said Fedrick, unable to think of anything.

Fedrick jumped off from the horse and the snake also fell at a distance. Salazar came and grasped the snake. First he got hold of its neck and then he pulled out one tooth from its mouth. He made sure that poison did not spread anywhere.

Salazar sighed as Fedrick looked on.

'It could have been hazardous, right' said Fedrick, surprised.

'Yes! But I did it' replied Salazar.

'It means that you also have powers' said Fedrick, excited.

Salazar nodded and said, 'Now let's continue our journey.'

CHAPTER-9

The Fedrick's Broom

Fedrick and Salazar were hungry. They started searching for something that could fulfill their hunger. Suddenly Fedrick , to his surprise, saw a biscuit house. 'Hey! Stop', said Fedrick.

'What happened', asked Salazar.

Fedrick pointed at the biscuit house.

'Wow' said Salazar and they glanced at each other.

They rode towards the biscuit house to eat the biscuits.While eating biscuits, Fedrick noticed something strange with the floor.He placed his hand on it and it creaked open.It had a secret tunnel.

'Salazar,it opens!'

Salazar came and saw.

'I think it's our next level. We have to jump in it' said Salazar.

'Then Jump!' said Fedrick and both of them jumped together .'Ahhhhhhhhhhhhh……………'they shouted.

Millennium brooms were scattered in the deep tunnel.

'Broomsticks' said Fedrick doubtfully.

'Wait a minute. There can be some flying brooms too' said Salazar.

'I just want to get up,' said Fedrick.

Suddenly, a broomstick came flying into his hands.

'I was right.Now we can get out of here too!' exclaimed Salazar after pausing for a few seconds.

CHAPTER–10

Goblin

They were scared to fly on a broomstick, so they first practiced. Their first try went in vain , when they said 'Up', the broom hit them on the face.Then after some time they were ready to get out of there.

'Let's take the brooms with us', said Fedrick.

'Okay' said Salazar politely.

Fedrick took two brooms and opened the door. Suddenly, Fedrick heard a laughing voice.

'Who is this fool now' said Fedrick.

'Which fool are you talking about ?' asked Salazar.

'I just heard a voice.' Said Fedrick.

Fedrick glanced up for a minute.

Then he saw a yellowish looking goblin flying with the help of a glider. The goblin threw a sphere shaped bomb. The attack was so sudden that as soon as the bomb touched the ground, it blasted and Fedrick's one life was gone.

Fedrick returned with life gone.

'We have to fly on the broom, that is the only way we can survive' said Fedrick.

'Yes' replied Salazar.

Fedrick grasped the broom and started flying.

'Ha Ha!, danger boys' laughed the Goblin.

'Let's see then!' challenged Fedrick.

Fedrick was flying as fast as he could. The goblin was throwing bombs and blades on him.

Goblin said, 'I will cut you in little pieces boy!'

Fedrick gave no answer , but was focused on flying. Then suddenly a ball-like substance hit his broom and Fedrick lost control. He fell off. Fedrick hit the ground but he was not dead. When he stood up, he was not able to see anything, a blindness surrounded him.

'Hey Salazar ! Where is the goblin?' said Fedrick confused.

'Can't you see him?' asked Salazar doubtfully.

'No' replied Fedrick.

'You are blind!' said Salazar.

'Ha Ha! Now I'll finish you', the goblin shouted.

'*Pushback!*' muttered Salazar and the goblin was falling too. But his glider had Artificial Intelligence and it came to save him.

'*Vanishium!*' muttered Salazar and the glider suddenly vanished.

'What is happening!' asked Fedrick.

'I am fighting the goblin' replied Salazar.

Then suddenly Fedrick vanished too but again appeared back.

'You are standing right behind the goblin' said Salazar.

'My power' said Fedrick.

'You are now gone boy' said the goblin.

'You are gone, you know' said Fedrick. '*Avra ka Davra!*'

A few seconds later, the goblin got extinct.

'You did it Fedrick!' exclaimed Salazar.

'Yeah! We did it!' exclaimed Fedrick smiling.

CHAPTER-11

The Zombies and the Eye

'Have I killed the Goblin?' asked Fedrick.

'Yes' replied Salazar.

'I am fed up with this game. Can we go home now? We've already completed these stupid adventures' said Fedrick. There was a pause for a few seconds.

> ' Loads of adventures done
> One adventure left
> If completed
> Say its name
> But remember
> Thick and Blue,
> Tried and True,
> Thin and Crispy,
> Way too risky '

'What is that sound in the air ?' asked Fedrick.

'I Dunno' said Salazar,' Hey, and what about your eye? Is it recovered or still....'asked Salazar.

'No.I still feel like concussion' replied Fedrick.

'Concussion!' exclaimed Salazar.

'Okay!I know what to do. Yes. In this game , if anyone gets hurt like you, we have to use these tea leaves.'said Salazar.

'Oh!' said Fedrick.

Salazar took out the tea leaves from his pocket and said, 'Here, take it and put it on your eyes for 1 minute.' said Salazar.

'Gentleman, how can I see one minute?'asked Fedrick.

'You have an option to guess', replied Salazar.

'Oh! I see' said Fedrick.

'But you always knew that you have tea leaves in your pocket' asked Fedrick.

'Yes,I knew' replied Salazar nodding.

'And you gave me tea leaves now,' said Fedrick, raising his eyebrows.

'Oh! Sorry! Now you can take off the tea leaves from your eyes' said Salazar.

Fedrick took off the tea leaves and blinked his eyes two times.

'Can you see now ?' asked Salazar.

'Yes ! I can see, Thank You Salazar' said elated Fedrick.

'And Salazar, I wanted to ask you something,' said Fedrick.

'Yes, Say.' Said Salazar.

'Are you Non Player Character of this game?' asked Fedrick

'No! My full name is Salazar Nikes and I got stuck in this game when a letter pranked me into this game' said Salazar.

'Never mind, Let's keep going' said Fedrick.

Suddenly they heard a sound, *Thud Thud !*

'Hey Salazar, can you feel it ?' asked Fedrick.

'I can see too' gasped Salazar.

Fedrick turned his head and saw an army of Zombies coming towards them.

'This is the time to use our broom sticks' said Fedrick.

'Nope,I am not flying with you' replied Salazar.

'You have to! If you don't want to die' insisted Fedrick.

'The zombies are coming nearer, you go' screamed Salazar.

'No way' said Fedrick.

Fedrick took Salazar's hand and suddenly disappeared. Now they were hovering in the sky.

'Ahhhhhhhh……….., we will diiiieeee' screamed Salazar.

'What are we doing in the sky' asked Salazar.

'I am flying ! It seems I can fly now as my new power in this game' exclaimed Fedrick.

'But where is your wand ?' asked Salazar.

'In my pocket' replied Fedrick, taking it out of his pocket.

But suddenly Fedrick lost his hold on his wand and the wand slipped from his hands.

'Oh no ! What did I do' said Fedrick.

'But they can't do anything to us, small little zombies' said Fedrick confidently.

'Wait, are they going to throw something on us' said Salazar doubtfully.

Suddenly a zombie threw something and it blasted.

'Damn it, these are bombs! Run !' said Fedrick.

'You just said the incorrect word, you should have said, Fly!' said Salazar.

'Ok! Flyyyyyyy…'.Then Fedrick flew away with Salazar. Zombies continued throwing bombs.

'Well, I never expected that zombies can throw bombs also,' said Fedrick.

'Don't lose control of yourself or we both will fall down.' Said Salazar

'Ok,stop your words of wisdom and tell me do you have any idea how to get rid of it' asked Fedrick.

'Nope' replied Salazar.

Suddenly he spoke again after a minute of extreme silence, 'Oh, I got one idea.I don't think we have seen all the parts and powers of the biscuit house.We should find the house to get something' explained Salazar.

'Sounds like a plan. Lets go then'replied Fedrick.

Fedrick and Salazar were finding their way, hours and hours passed away .Finally they saw a big house.

'Hey! That is the house' exclaimed Salazar.

'No, it is not that house' replied Fedrick.

'We can just go once and see in there' suggested Salazar.

'Ok' replied Fedrick.

'Go!Go!Go! faster. The zombies are fortifying the house.' Said Salazar.

'Yes we made it' said Fedrick, as they entered the house.

'That is the trap door, let's go inside it' said Salazar

They entered the hall.

'Yes ! bombs and guns- with these we can defeat them' said Fedrick.

Fedrick and Salazar picked up bombs and a couple of guns.

'Now we are ready' said Fedrick.

'I'll aim towards the trap door, it will make a noise and zombies will hear it' intended Fedrick.

Fedrick did as planned, then zombies jumped into the trap door hearing the noise of gunshots. Some zombies died as they fell while others survived.

'So are you ready' said Fedrick.

'Yes' replied Salazar as they started firing gunshots at the zombies.

'Hey! Our bullets are finished' said Salazar after sometime.

'Let's fly out then' said Fedrick.

'Ok ! Flyyyyy....' said Fedrick.

Fedrick started flying and exited through the trapdoor.

'This is turning out to be a very long fight' said Fedrick.

'Yes, I have an idea, do you remember the song, Thick n Blue ?' asked Salazar

'Yes!' replied Fedrick.

'We have to sing that song and every zombie will be finished' said Salazar.

'Ok, Let's try it,' said Fedrick.

Thick and Blue !

Tried and True !

Thin and Crispy !

Way too risky !

Then zombies started disappearing one by one. After sometime all the zombies were gone.Then few lines appeared in the air

THE GRUDGE HAS

BEEN COMPLETED !

'Yes ! We completed the game, Wooooo…..' said Fedrick excitedly.

'Then why aren't we going home' said Salazar.

'We have to call out its name together' said Fedrick.

'But wait, before going could we say a formal Goodbye to each other' said Fedrick heartedly.

'Oh Yes! It was very pleasantly scary to pass through these adventures with you' replied Salazar. 'GoodBye Fedrick' he said.

'Goodbye Dear Salazar' said Fedrick.

'*TOMITARO*' screamed both of them.

Fedrick was back to his home now.

'I'am back home' said relieved Fedrick.

He went downstairs and saw his mom and dad in the kitchen. There was a policeman with them.

'Mom! Dad! I am back home' said Fedrick as he ran to hug them.

'Where have you been ?' asked his Dad as there were tears in his eyes.

'I'll explain later' relied' replied Fedrick.'What date it is' he asked.

'8th October, my child. You've been missing for a couple of days, ' replied his mother, holding her tears.

'I have been missing for two days' thought Fedrick. 'It was Saturday and Sunday ! Never mind'.

Fedrick slept tight that night as he destroyed the ring before going for sleep.